HarperCollins®, ☂®, and HarperEntertainment™ are trademarks of HarperCollins Publishers.
Monsters vs. Aliens: Save San Francisco
Monsters vs. Aliens™ & © 2009 DreamWorks Animation L.L.C.

www.harpercollinschildrens.com

Library of Congress catalog card number is available.
ISBN 978-0-06-156723-0

Book design by Joe Merkel
❖
First Edition

Whoosh! A bright light flashed against the night sky. Then a giant alien robot crashed to Earth!

"No one knows what it is or where it came from," said news reports. No one knew whether it was friendly or hostile, either.

Helicopters swarmed around the robot as the president of the United States attempted first contact. "This is about peaceful communication," said President Hathaway, shooing his secret service agents aside.

The president walked up a staircase to a keyboard and played a popular, welcoming melody. The robot extended his arm toward the president as if to shake hands, then—*BAM!*—smashed the instrument! It did not appreciate the music!

"Light 'em up!" an army commander ordered. The soldiers released a tidal wave of bullets, rockets, and missiles at the robot. But the bullets bounced off the robot's force field!

"Call in a full retreat!" said the commander. The military would not be able to stop the invader. It was time to call upon some very special secret weapons . . .

... MONSTERS! General Monger knew Earth's only chance for survival was the motley crew of mutants he kept in an ultra-secret prison: The Missing Link, an ancient fish-man; B.O.B., an indestructible mass; Dr. Cockroach, PhD, a mad scientist; and Insectosaurus, a giant bug.

There was also Ginormica, a young bride-to-be who was hit by a meteor and grew to be a whopping 49 feet, 11 inches tall! The monsters were ordered to succeed where the U.S. Army had failed.

The alien robot charged at Ginormica as she raced through San Francisco. B.O.B. tried to stop it. *Splat!* He stuck to the enormous robot's foot like a giant wad of gum. "I got him! Tell me it's slowing down!" he called out. But it wasn't!

Dr. Cockroach spotted an abandoned tram. "I have a plan!" said the scientist. "To the untrained eye, a tram is just a tram. But to a genius, it's the foundation for a turbo-powered vehicle!" Dr. Cockroach made fast work of overhauling.

Dr. Cockroach and The Missing Link chased after the rampaging robot. "I'm going to pull up alongside it. You get to its central processing unit," Dr. Cockroach ordered The Missing Link.

But B.O.B. foiled his friends' plans. "Hey guys, catch me!" he yelled, still stuck to the robot's foot. Then he splat all over the tram—causing it to crash into the water.

Meanwhile, the interstellar invader was still hot on Ginormica's trail. The sounds of the chase thundered through the deserted city, where the robot crashed through building after building.

Ginormica smashed her feet through a pair of convertible cars, and skated out of the battered city onto the Golden Gate Bridge. "Excuse me! Coming through!" Ginormica bellowed.

The alien continued chasing Ginormica and crashed right through the side of the bridge! Cars and trucks began sliding toward the water far below.

"No, no, no! Get away from me!" Ginormica yelled. She fought as hard as she could to keep out of the robot's enormous claws.

Amid this panic, Insectosaurus came to the rescue! The enormous grub shot silk fibers into the robot's eye, blinding it and giving Ginormica just enough time to escape the robot's clutches.

With B.O.B.'s help, Ginormica brought the commuters to safety while Dr. Cockroach fiddled with the robot's wires. "You can't crush a cockroach! *Mua ha ha ha ha!*" the doctor laughed.

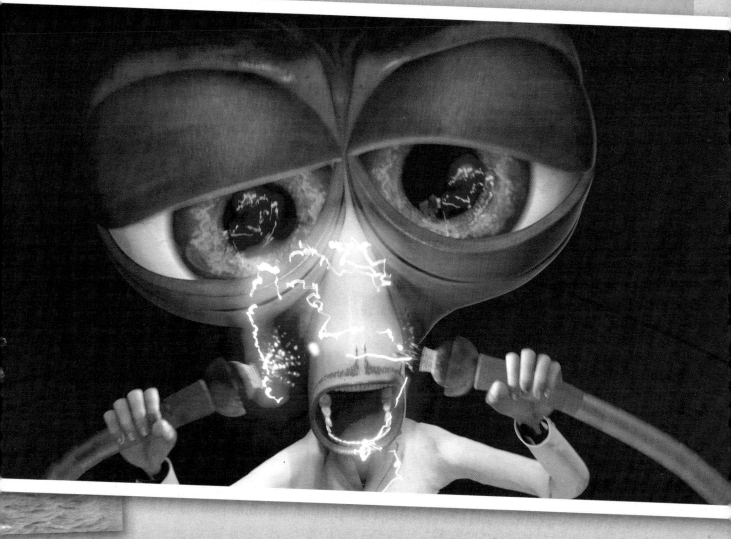

Ginormica knew it was up to her to stop the robot. She grabbed
loose cables from the bridge, swinging them around and around
the alien robot's arms. Ginormica heaved with all her strength.
"I got this!" she hollered.

The gigantic robot finally came crashing down. Massive amounts of steel and concrete from the battered bridge smashed onto the machine—stopping it for good!

Ginormica, Dr. Cockroach, The Missing Link, B.O.B., and Insectosaurus had done it! They had saved San Francisco. Now they weren't just monsters. They were heroes!